Chapter Two

ALL NIGHT, AS the storm raged outside, the birds in the barn huddled together in their nests, burying their heads in each other to blot out the sound of the thunder. The wind whined and whistled through the eaves, the walls shuddered and the beams creaked and groaned. But Screecher and Colly were not worried. They'd been through storms like this before and the old barn had held together.

Screecher thought the worst of it was over. He was peering through a crack in the wall, looking for the first light of dawn on the distant hills, when the lightning struck. In one blinding flash night was turned to day. A deafening clap of thunder shook the barn and a fireball glowing orange and blue rolled around the barn and disappeared through the door.

Through the smoke Screecher could see that the crack in the wall was suddenly a gaping hole and above him the roof was open to the rain.

Grandad's bad knee kept him in bed the next morning and Annie was at school when her father and mother discovered the hole in the barn wall.

'Lucky it didn't catch fire,' said Annie's mother.

'Might have been better if it had,' said her father. 'One way or another that barn's got to come down now. I've been saying it for years.'

'You could patch it up,' Annie's mother replied.

Her father shook his head. 'Waste of time and money. New modern shed, that's what we need. I'll have a bulldozer in, we'll soon have it down.'

'Grandad won't like it,' she said. 'You know how much he likes the old buildings. I don't want you upsetting him again.'

'It's just a tumbledown old barn,' he said.
'Anyway, Grandad won't know till it's all over.
He won't be out of bed for a couple of days,
not with his knee like it is. And not a word to
Annie, she tells him everything. Thick as thieves
they are, those two.'

High above them in the old barn, Screecher
and Colly were perched side by side listening
to every word. 'What'll we do?' said Screecher.
'There's nowhere else to nest for miles around;
and even if there was, my two children won't

be ready to fly for
another month or more.
I can't move them and I
won't leave them. I won't.'
Colly said nothing. She
flew off to join the swifts and
housemartins as they skimmed low
over the high grass in Long Meadow. The
message that Screecher and his family were in
trouble soon got around. At first some of them
refused to help. There was a rumour that
Screecher had killed a cock robin not so long
ago. The sparrows and the crows, and there
were a lot of them, said that it was nothing to
do with them, that everyone had to look after
themselves. But all the birds that lived in the
barn, the fan-tailed doves, the swallows, the
swifts, and the little wren, needed no
persuading. After all they'd seen
Screecher, only the day before,
diving down to rescue
Colly's fledgling
from the cat.

'I've got babies in my nest just like Screecher,' said the wren. 'And anyway, if they knock down the barn where are we going to nest next year and the year after that?'

All day long the birds argued, and it was almost dark before they were all agreed at last. 'Then we'll start work at first light tomorrow,' said Colly. 'Let's all get some sleep.'

Chapter Three

THE NEXT MORNING Grandad looked out
from his bedroom window at the crowd of
birds swirling around the barn. 'They must be
after the flies in the thatch,' he said to Annie's
mother when she brought him his early
morning tea.

'Who knows,' she said. 'You just stay in bed
and rest that knee of yours.'

Annie sat down to breakfast in the kitchen.
'There's swarms of birds out there,' she said.
'Like bees. What're they up to?'

'Who knows,' said her father. 'Eat up, you'll
be late for school.'

As she got off the school bus that afternoon Annie could see the birds still soaring and swooping around the barn. She ran up the lane to get a closer look. Grandad was there in his dressing-gown. 'I wouldn't have thought it possible,' he said. 'You see that hole in the wall? Must have happened in the storm. They're mending it, that's what they're doing.'

As Annie watched she saw the swifts and swallows and housemartins come flying in with mud in their beaks. They fluttered briefly at the

wall and flew off again. The crows and
buzzards hovered over the roof before landing
with their twigs and straw, and the wren darted
to and fro, her beak full of moss and lichen.
'Your father's not going to believe this,' said
Grandad.

And he was right. He didn't. Nor did her
mother. They wouldn't even come out to look.

'You'll catch your death, Grandad,' Annie's
mother said. 'Back to bed with you now.'

Annie tried to tell them but they wouldn't
listen to her either. They didn't want to hear
another word about the barn or the birds, not
one word.

'You'll tire yourself out, Colly,' said Screecher
that night.

'Don't you worry,' Colly said. 'These wings
have taken me to Africa and back five times
now, they'll carry me a lot further yet. A few
more days and the barn will be as good as new
again and then they won't need to knock it
down, will they?'

'We need more help with the roof,' said
Screecher. 'I'll fly down to the river tomorrow
and ask the herons. They're the experts.'

But Colly didn't even hear him, she was fast
asleep.

Chapter Four

ANNIE WANTED TO be quite sure Grandad
was right, so all weekend she stayed and she
watched the birds flying back and forth. Even
Screecher was out flying by day and she'd
never seen that before. He was fetching and
carrying just like all the others. Of all of them
though, it was the swallows, and one of them
in particular, that worked hardest, swooping
down to the muddy puddles and up to the
barn wall with never a pause for rest. Annie
knew now for certain that Grandad had not
been imagining things.

'It's true,' she said. 'What Grandad says, it's
all true.' But they still wouldn't believe her.
When she shouted at them she was sent off
to bed early. Grandad came to comfort her.

'There's none so blind as them that won't see,' he said. Annie wasn't sure what he meant by that.

He told her one of his hobgoblin stories, but she could think only of Screecher and the birds in the barn.

She wasn't at all surprised then to see Screecher fly into her dream. He flew in through the window and perched on the end of her bed. There was something in his beak. He let it fall

on her bedcover. She sat up to get a closer
look. It was a dead swallow.

'He's going to knock down the barn,' said
Screecher.

'Who is?' said Annie.

'Your father. We heard him, Colly and me.'

'Colly?'

'That's Colly lying on your bed,' Screecher
said. 'I tried to tell her, I told her she'd kill
herself if she worked so hard. She never stopped
– all day and every day. We've got to finish it,
she said, and then they won't have to knock
down our home.'

'Home?' said Annie.

'That barn is our home. We've got nowhere else to live. You've got to stop him. You've got to tell your father or else he'll bring in the bulldozer.'

'But he won't believe me,' said Annie. 'He doesn't believe anything I say. You tell him. He'll believe you, he'll listen to you.' And Screecher was suddenly gone.

It's a funny thing about dreams, they always seem to finish just as you wake up. There was a rumbling outside Annie's window, and voices.

She sat up and looked out. Her father was standing by a great yellow bulldozer that belched black smoke and he was pointing up at the barn. Annie looked down and saw the swallow lying on her bed. She picked it up. Colly was limp in her hand, her beak half open. Annie never bothered with slippers or her dressing gown. She ran crying out of the house. Grandad heard her and her mother heard her. Her father heard nothing until the driver of the bulldozer switched off his engine and pointed at Annie as she came running up the path. Her father looked at the swallow in her hand.

'That's Colly isn't it?' he said.

Annie looked at him amazed. 'You know?' she said.

'I had a visitor last night,' he said. He told me everything, Annie. He brought me out here to show me the hole they'd mended. When I woke up this morning I thought I'd been sleepwalking, so I came and had another look. I wasn't dreaming, Annie.'

'Neither was I,' said Annie.

Grandad came puffing up the path, with
Mother behind him. 'What's going on?' said
Grandad. 'What's that bulldozer for?'

'Oh, nothing,' said Annie's father. 'Just took
a wrong turning somewhere, that's all. Lost his
way. We all do that from time to time, don't we
Grandad?'

They buried Colly that morning in the
corner of Long Meadow under the great ash
tree. If Annie had looked up she'd have seen
Screecher perched high above her, half hidden
by the leaves, Colly's fledgling beside him.
And they weren't alone. Every branch,
every twig of the tree was lined with
silent birds.

Michael Morpurgo

C NKER

Illustrated by Gerry Turley

Chapter One

MOST DOGS HAVE one name, but Pooch had three – one after the other. Pooch was what Grandma called him in the first place. But when Nick was a toddler he couldn't say Pooch very well and so Pooch soon became Pooh.

Then one day Pooh heard the rattle of the milk bottles outside and came bounding out of the house to say hello to the milkman – he liked the milkman. But today it was a different one. Pooh prowled around him sniffing at the bottom of his trousers. The new milkman went as white as his milk. Nick tried to drag Pooh back into the house, but he wouldn't come.

"S'like a wolf,' said the milkman, putting his hands on his head and backing down the path. 'You ought to chain it up.'

'Not a wolf,' Nick said. 'He's an old station.'

'A what?' said the milkman.

'An old station,' Nick said. 'Pooh is an old station.' At that moment Grandma came to the door.

'Nick gets his words muddled sometimes,' she said. 'He's only little. I think he means an *Alsatian*, don't you, dear? Old Station! Old Station! You are a funny boy, Nick.' And she laughed so much that she nearly cried. So from that day Pooh was called Old Station.

There were always just the three of them in the house. Nick had lived with Grandma for as long as he could remember. She looked after Nick, and Old Station looked after them both.

Everywhere they went Old Station went with them. 'Don't know what we'd do without him,' Grandma would say.

All his life Old Station had been like a big brother to Nick. Nick was nine years old now. He had watched Old Station grow old as he grew up. The old dog moved slowly these days, and when he got up in the morning to go outside you could see it was a real effort. He would spend most of the day asleep in his basket, dreaming his dreams.

Nick watched him that morning as he ate his cornflakes before he went off to school. It was the last day before half-term. Old Station was growling in his sleep as he often did and his whiskers were twitching.

'He's chasing cats in his dreams,' said Grandma. 'Hurry up, Nick, else you'll be late.' She gave him his satchel and packed lunch, and Nick called out 'Goodbye' to Old Station and ran off down the road.

It was a windy autumn morning with the leaves

falling all around him. Before he got to school
he caught twenty-six of them in mid-air and that
was more than he'd ever caught before. By the
end of the day the leaves were piled as high as
his ankles in the gutters, and Nick scuffled
through them on the way back home, thinking

of all the bike rides he could go on now that half-term had begun.

Old Station wasn't there to meet him at the door as he sometimes was, and Grandma wasn't in the kitchen cooking tea as she usually was. Old Station wasn't in his basket either.

Nick found Grandma in the back garden, taking the washing off the line. 'Nice windy day. Wanted to leave the washing out as long as possible,' she said from behind the sheet. 'I'll get your tea in a minute, dear.'

'Where's Old Station?' Nick said. 'He's not in his basket.'

Grandma didn't reply, not at first anyway; and when she did Nick wished she never had done.

'He had to go,' Grandma said simply, and she walked past him without even looking at him.

'Go where?' Nick asked, 'What do you mean? Where's he gone to?'

Grandma put the washing down on the kitchen table and sat down heavily in the chair. Nick could see then that she'd been crying, and he knew that Old Station was dead.

'The Vet said he was suffering,' she said, looking up at him. 'We couldn't have him suffering, could we? It had to be done. That's all there is to it. Just a pinprick it was, dear, and then he went off to sleep. Nice and peaceful.'

'He's dead then,' Nick said.

Grandma nodded. 'I buried him outside in the garden by the wall. It's what was best for him, Nick,' she said. 'You know that don't you?' Nick nodded and they cried quietly together.

After tea Grandma put Old Station's basket out in the shed and showed Nick where she had buried him. 'We'll plant something over him, shall we, dear?' she said. 'A rose perhaps, so we won't forget him.'

'We'll never forget him,' said Nick. 'Never.'

Chapter Two

THE DAY AFTER Old Station died was Saturday.
Saturdays and Sundays in the conker season
meant conkers in Jubilee Park with his friends,
but Nick didn't feel like seeing anyone, not that
day. Every time he looked out of the
kitchen window into the back
garden he felt like crying. It was
Grandma's idea that he should go
for a long ride, and so he did.
The next best thing in the world
after Old Station was the bike
Grandma had given him on his

birthday. It was shining royal blue with three-speed gears, a bell, a front light and everything. Just to sit on it made him feel happy. By the time he got back from his ride he felt a lot better.

The next morning Nick went off to Jubilee Park as he always did on a Sunday. All his friends were there, and so was Stevie Rooster. Stevie Rooster called himself the 'Conker King of Jubilee Park'. He was one of those bragging brutish boys who could hit harder, run faster and shout louder than anyone else. There was only one thing Stevie had ever been frightened of, and that was Old Station. Perhaps it was because of Old Station that Nick was the one boy he had never bullied.

Of course they all knew about Old Station, but no one said anything about him, except for Stevie Rooster. 'So that smelly old dog of yours kicked the bucket at last,' he said. Perhaps he was expecting everyone to laugh, but no one did.

Nick tried to stop himself from crying.

Stevie went on, ''Bout time if you ask me.'

In his fury Nick tore the conker out of Stevie Rooster's hand and hurled it into the pond.

'That's my twenty-fiver,' Stevie bellowed, and he lashed out at Nick with his fist, catching him in the mouth.

Nick looked at the blood on the back of his hand and flew at Stevie's throat like an alley cat. In the end Nick was left with a split lip, a black eye and a torn shirt. He was lucky to get away with just that. If the Park Keeper had not come along when he did it might have been a lot worse.

Grandma shook her head as she bathed his face in the kitchen. 'What does it matter what Stevie Rooster says about Old Station?' she said. 'Look what he's done to you. Look at your face.'

'I had to get him,' Nick said.

'But you didn't, did you? I mean he's bigger than you isn't he? He's twice your size and nasty with it. If you want to beat him, you've got to use your head. It's the only way.'

'What do you mean, Grandma?' Nick asked. 'What else could I do?'

'Conkers,' said Grandma. Didn't you tell me once that he likes to call himself the "Conker King of Jubilee Park"?'

'Yes.'

'Well then,' said Grandma. 'You've got to knock him off his throne, haven't you?'

'But how?'

'You've got to beat him at conkers,' she said. 'And I'm going to teach you how. There's nothing I don't know about conkers, Nick, nothing. You'll see.'

Chapter Three

SOMEHOW NICK HAD never thought of his Grandma as a conker expert.

'First we must find the right conkers,' she said. 'And there's only one place to find a champion conker and that's from the old conker tree out by Cotter's Yard. It's still standing, I saw it from the bus only the other day. I never had a conker off that tree that let me down. Always hard as nails they are. Mustn't be any bigger than my thumbnail. Small and hard is what we're after.'

And so it was that Nick found himself that

afternoon cycling along the road out of town, past the football ground and the gasworks, with a packet of jelly babies in his pocket. 'Now don't eat them all at once, dear,' Grandma had told him. 'Go carefully and look for the tree on the left-hand side of the road just as you come to Cotter's Yard; you know, the scrapyard where they crunch up old cars. You can't miss it.'

And Grandma's conker tree was just where she said it was, a great towering conker tree standing on its own by the scrapyard.

Nick must have spent half an hour searching through the leaves under the tree, but he couldn't find a single conker. He was about to give up and go home when he spotted a cluster of prickly green balls lying in the long grass on the other side of the fence. There was no sign of life in Cotter's Yard. No one would be there on a Sunday afternoon. No one would mind if he went in just to pick up conkers. There was nothing wrong with that, he thought.

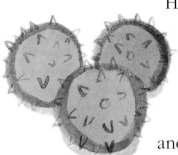

He climbed quickly. At the top he swung his legs over and dropped down easily on the other side. He found the cluster of three small conkers and broke them open. Each one was shining brown and perfect, and just the right size. He stuffed them into his pocket and was just about to climb out again when he heard from somewhere behind him in Cotter's Yard, the distant howling of a dog. His first thought was to scramble up over the fence and escape, but then the howling stopped and the dog began to whine and whimper and yelp. It was a cry for help which Nick could not ignore.

Cotter's Yard was a maze of twisted rusting wrecks. The muddy tracks through it were littered with car tyres. Great piles of cars towered all about him now as he picked his way round the potholes. And all the while the pitiful howling echoed louder around him. He was getting closer.

He found the guard dog sitting by a hut in the centre of the Yard. He was chained by the neck to a metal stake, and he was shivering so much that his teeth were rattling. The chain was twisted over his back and wrapped around his back legs so that he could not move. 'Doesn't look ferocious,' Nick thought, 'but you never know.' And he walked slowly around the guard dog at a safe distance.

And then Nick noticed the dog's face. It was as
if Old Station had come back from the grave and
was looking up at him. He had the same gentle
brown eyes, the same way of holding his head
on one side when he was thinking. Old Station
liked jelly babies, Nick thought. Perhaps
this one will. One by one the dog
took them gently out of Nick's
hand, chewed them,
swallowed them and then
waited for the next one.

When there were no more Nick gave him the paper bag to play with whilst he freed him from the chain. He ate the bag too, and when he stood up and shook himself, Nick could see that he was thin like a greyhound is thin. There were sores around his neck behind his ears where his collar had rubbed him raw.

Nick sat down beside him, took off his duffel coat and rubbed him and rubbed him until his teeth stopped chattering. He didn't like to leave him, but it was getting dark. 'Don't worry,' Nick said, walking away. The dog followed him to the end of his chain. 'I'll be back,' he said. 'I promise I will.' Nick knew now exactly what he wanted to do, but he had no idea at all how he was going to do it.

It was dark by the time Nick got home and Grandma was not pleased with him. 'Where have you been? I was worried sick about you,' she said, taking off his coat and shaking it out.

'The conkers were difficult to find, Grandma,' Nick said, but he said no more.

Grandma was pleased with the conkers though. 'Just like they always were,' she said, turning them over in her hands. 'Unbreakable little beauties.' And then Grandma began what she called her 'conker magic'. First she put them in the oven for exactly twelve minutes. Then she took them out and dropped them still hot into a pudding basin full of her conker potion: a mixture of vinegar, salt, mustard and a teaspoon

1. Vinegar

2. Salt

of Worcester Sauce. One hour later she took them out again and put them back into the oven for another twelve minutes. When they came out they were dull and crinkled. She polished them with furniture polish till they shone again. Then she drove a small brass nail through the conkers one after the other and examined each one carefully. She put two of them aside and held up the third in triumph.

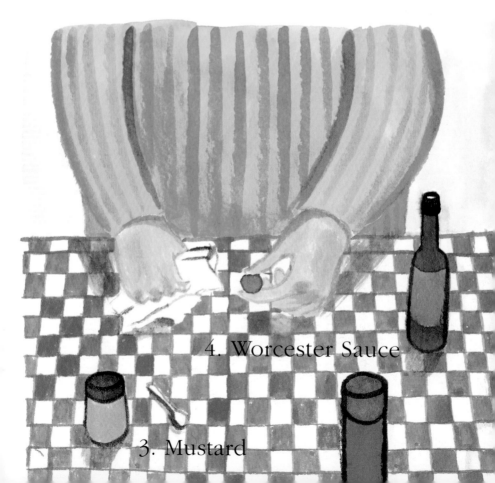

4. Worcester Sauce

3. Mustard

'This is the one,' she said. 'This is your champion conker. All you have to do now, Nick, is sleep with that down the bottom of your bed tonight and tomorrow you'll be "Conker King of Jubilee Park".'

But Nick couldn't sleep that night. He lay there thinking of the dog he had left behind in Cotter's Yard, and about how he was going to rescue him. By breakfast the next morning he was still not sure how to set about it.

'Remember, you must play on a short

string,' Grandma was saying. 'And always play on grass so it won't break if he pulls it out of your hand. And try not to get tangled up - puts a strain on the knot. What's the matter with you, dear? You're not eating your breakfast.'

'Grandma,' Nick said, 'what if you found a dog all chained up and lonely and miserable, would you try to rescue it?'

'What makes you ask a thing like that, dear?' Grandma said.

'Would you?' Nick asked.

'Of course, dear.'

'Even if it meant stealing it, Grandma?'

'Ah well, that's different. Two wrongs don't make a right, Nick,' she said. 'What's all this about?'

'Oh nothing, nothing,' Nick said quickly. 'I was just thinking, that's all.'

Nick could feel she was suspicious. He had said far too much already. He left quickly before she could ask any more questions.

'Good luck, Nick,' Grandma called after him as he went off down the path.

He cycled right up to Stevie Rooster in the
Park and challenged him there and then. 'I've
got a conker that'll beat any conker you've got,'
he said. Stevie Rooster laughed at Nick and his
little conker, but when his first conker broke in
two the smile left his face. He took conker after
conker out of his sack, and each one was
shattered into little pieces within seconds. A

crowd gathered as
Nick's conker became a twentier,
a thirtier, a fiftier and then at last an eighty-fiver.
Stevie Rooster's face was red with fury as he
took his last conker out of his sack.

'Your turn,' Nick said quietly and he held up
his conker. There still wasn't a mark on it. Stevie
swung again and was left holding a piece of

empty string with a knot swinging at the end of it. Nick looked him in the face and saw the tears of humiliation start into his eyes. 'You shouldn't have said that about Old Station,' Nick said and he turned, got on his bike and cycled off leaving a stunned crowd behind him.

Chapter Four

IT WAS A twenty minute ride up to Cotter's
Yard, but Nick did it in ten. All through the
conker game he had been thinking about it and
now at last he knew what to do. He had a plan.
He was breathless by the time he got there. The
gates were wide open. The Yard was working
today, the great crane swinging out over the
crushing machine, a car hanging from its jaws.

'Hey you, what're you after?' It was a voice
from the door of the hut. It belonged to a
weasel-faced man with mean little eyes.

'I've come to buy your dog,' Nick said. 'Haven't got any money, but I'll swop my bike for your dog. It's almost new, three speed and everything. Had it for my birthday, a month ago.' Nick looked around for the dog, but there was no sign of him. The chain lay curled up in the mud by the hut.

'Haven't got no dog here,' said the weasel-faced man, 'not any more. Wasn't any use anyway. Got rid of him, didn't I?'

'What do you mean?' Nick said.

'Just what I said. I got rid of him. Vet came and took him away this morning. No use to me he wasn't. Now push off out of here.' And he went back inside the hut and slammed the door behind him.

As Nick cycled home, the rain came spitting down through the trees. He had never felt more miserable in his life. When Old Station died he had been sad enough, but this was different and much, much worse. This had been his fault. If only he had come back earlier, if only. By the time he reached home he was blinded with tears.

'Well, and how's the "Conker King of Jubilee Park"?' Grandma called out from the kitchen as he closed the door behind him, and she came hurrying out to meet him. 'Well I told you, didn't I? I told you. It's all down the street. Everyone knows my Nick's the Conker King. Well, come on, let's see the famous conker. An eighty-fiver, isn't it?'

'Eighty-sixer,' Nick said and burst into tears against her apron.

'What's all this?' Grandma said, putting her arm round him and leading him into the kitchen. 'We can't have the "Conker King of Jubilee Park" crying his eyes out.' And Nick blurted it all out, all about Cotter's Yard and the poor starving dog he had found there that looked just like Old Station, about how the vet had come and taken him away.

'I was going to buy him for you with my bike,' Nick said, 'to take Old Station's place, but I was too late.'

'Who says you were?' said Grandma, and there was a certain tone in her voice.

'What do you mean?' Nick asked.

'What I mean, dear, is that if you'd wipe your eyes and look over in the corner there, you'd see a basket with a dog in it, and if you looked hard at that dog you might just recognise him.'

Nick looked. The dog from Cotter's Yard lay curled up in Old Station's basket, his great brown eyes gazing up at him. The dog got up, stretched, yawned and came over to him.

'But how . . . ?' Nick began.

Grandma held up her hand.

'When you came home from Cotter's Yard yesterday with your duffel coat stinking of dog, I was a little suspicious. You see, old Cotter's known for the cruel way he looks after his guard dogs, always has been. And then when you asked me this morning if I would rescue a dog if I found him all chained up and hungry and miserable - well, I put two and two together.'

'But he said the Vet came and took him away - he told me,' Nick said.

'So he did, dear, so he did. We went out there together, the vet and me, and we made old Cotter an offer he couldn't refuse. Either we took his dog with us or we reported him for cruelty to animals. Didn't take him long to make up his mind, I can tell you.'

'So he's ours then, Grandma?' Nick said.

'Yours, Nick, he's yours. Old Station was mine. I had him even before I had you, remember? But this one's yours, your prize for winning the Conker Championship of Jubilee Park. Now can I see that famous conker or can't I?'

Nick fished the conker out of his pocket and held it up by the string. Before he knew it, the dog had jumped up and jerked it out of his hand. A few seconds later all that was left was a mass of wet crumbs and chewed string.

'It looks as if he likes conkers for his tea,' Grandma said.

'Better call him "Conker" then,' Nick said. And so they did.

MICHAEL MORPURGO

Jo-Jo
the
Melon Donkey

Illustrated by Tony Kerins

Chapter One

JO-JO WAS A donkey. His father had been a
donkey before him, and his mother as well.
And so, of course, Jo-Jo had to be a donkey
whether he liked it or not. And he did not like
it, not one bit.

Work began early every morning for Jo-Jo.
First, his master would load him with so many
melons that he could hardly walk. Then he
would drive him out of the village and down
the dusty road towards the great city of Venice.

Jo-Jo loved Venice. It was his city. He loved the canals and the bridges, and the little squares and the sound of the church bells ringing out over the rooftops. He loved to stand and watch the water lapping around the houses, almost as if it wanted to suck the city back into the sea.

All day long his master would haul him down the narrow footpaths that ran alongside the canals, and Jo-Jo would call out, 'Melons. Melons. Melons for sale!' His braying would echo down the canals and into the squares. Everyone would know it was Jo-Jo, the melon donkey, and come running with their money. And all the while the flies came to torment him and would not go away.

Only in the cool of the evening resting under his olive tree, were there no flies to bother him and no master to bully him. Then at last he could be at peace. He would roll blissfully in his patch of dust, shake himself happy and lie down to dream.

Chapter Two

ONE MISTY SUMMER sunrise his master woke him as usual.

'Up, up, up, you old ragbag,' he shouted. 'No more little back streets for me. I'm going up in the world. I've heard they'll pay double for melons in St Mark's Square – that's where the rich folks live. Even the Doge, the ruler of Venice himself, might buy one of my melons.'

The load was even heavier that morning, but Jo-Jo didn't mind. He had a sudden feeling inside him that something good was about to happen.

By the time they reached St Mark's Square,
the sun was high in the sky and the square was
already full of people.

'Don't know why I never thought of this
before,' said his master, unloading the melons.

98

'This is the place for us, right in front of the Cathedral. We'll sell them all in no time. Sing out, you old ragbag you, sing out.'

'Melons. Melons. Melons for sale!' Jo-Jo brayed, and his cry rang around the square.

Everyone in St Mark's Square stopped and turned and looked. And then one of them began to laugh, and then another and another until the entire square was filled with laughter.

'What are you laughing at?' asked Jo-Jo's master. 'You've seen a donkey before, haven't you? What's so funny?'

'Above your head,' they cried. 'Look above your head!' Jo-Jo and his master looked up. Behind them, glowing in the sun, stood the four golden horses of Venice, the four most beautiful horses in all the world. 'Beauty and the beast!' roared the crowd. 'Beauty and the beast.' Jo-Jo hung his head in shame.

All morning the people came to point and stare, but they bought no melons. 'Take your donkey to the back streets, where he belongs,' they said. 'And you can take your melons too. We don't eat melons here. They're not for the likes of us.'

Then, as noon chimed, the great doors of the Doge's Palace opened and a little girl ran out into St Mark's Square, a nurse bustling after her.

'Come back, come back,' the nurse cried. 'You know you're not allowed out of the palace.'

'But I want a melon,' said the little girl. 'And anyway I don't like being cooped up in that palace all day. I've got no friends to play with and I'm bored.'

'It's the Doge's daughter,' someone whispered; and soon everyone was there, bowing and curtseying as she passed. She ignored them all and made straight for the pile of melons beside Jo-Jo.

'How much do you want for one of your melons?' she asked Jo-Jo's master.

'Such an honour, Highness. Such an honour,' replied Jo-Jo's master. 'For Your Highness, it's a gift. I have the best melons in all of Venice, Highness, and this one is for you.'

'Thank you,' said the Doge's daughter, taking
the melon; and then she noticed Jo-Jo standing
beside his master.

'He has such sad, kind eyes,' she said. And
she reached out and stroked Jo-Jo on his neck.
Jo-Jo had never been patted in all his life, and
his knees weakened with joy.

'Really, Your Highness,' said the nurse, taking the Doge's daughter by the arm. 'Fancy touching that filthy creature. Can't you see there are flies all over him? Come along back to the palace before your father sees you.' And she hustled the little girl away.

Jo-Jo closed his eyes and held the picture of the little girl in his mind so that it would never go away.

Within a few minutes all the melons were
sold. Suddenly anyone who was anyone in St
Mark's Square was eating melons. After all, what
was good enough for the Doge's daughter was
good enough for them.

So every day that summer, Jo-Jo came to
St Mark's Square loaded with melons and
stood under the four golden horses in front
of the Cathedral. And every day the Doge's
daughter came at noon for her melon. And
every time she came, she never failed to smile
at Jo-Jo. She would always talk gently to him
and smooth his nose before she left.

Chapter Three

ONE AFTERNOON, WHILE his master dozed under his hat and the whole city slumbered through the heat of the day, Jo-Jo was gazing up at the four shining golden horses in St Mark's Square, as he often did. They were everything the donkey longed to be but never could be.

'Oh, why can't I be like you?' he cried.

His master woke from his snoring sleep and beat him.

'How dare you wake me like that?' he roared.
'No use talking to those horses. Can't you see
they're nothing but statues? Statues can't hear.
Statues can't speak.'

But Jo-Jo knew they could.

The very next morning, just after Jo-Jo and
his master arrived in the square, the Great Doge
came to the window of his palace. Trumpets
sounded and a crowd gathered to listen.

'Be it known to one and all,' said the Doge,
'that I intend to purchase the finest horse in
the city for my daughter's birthday. A price of
ten thousand ducats will be paid. The horse
will be chosen at noon this very day, for
today is my daughter's birthday. Let the bells
ring out!'

All that morning Jo-Jo stood and watched
the horses arriving in the square. Every one of
them was finer than the one before and every
one of them made him feel smaller and uglier
than ever. There were black Arabian stallions
with tossing heads, snorting as they came.
There were grey Spanish mares with flowing
manes, prancing as they came. Soon all the
finest horses in the city were there, and a huge
crowd had gathered.

As the noon bell sounded, the great Doge

came out into the square with his daughter, and the grand parade began. The crowd clapped and cheered as all the horses trotted by.

Then all of Venice waited silently to hear his choice.

'My daughter is ten years old today,' he said, 'so she is quite old enough to choose for herself.' He turned to his daughter.

'Now my child,' he said, 'which one would you like?'

The Doge's daughter walked slowly along the line of waiting horses, and then at last she turned away and pointed. 'Over there!' she said, pointing towards the four golden horses.

'But you can't have them,' laughed the Doge, 'you can't have the golden horses. They belong to the people of Venice. They've been there for hundreds of years.'

'Not them,' the Doge's daughter said. 'I want that one over there, the one that's standing by the melons, Father.'

The crowd gasped.

'But that's a donkey! You want a donkey?' the Doge cried.

'Yes, Father,' said the Doge's daughter.

'I forbid it,' said the Doge, 'I absolutely forbid it. I cannot have a daughter of mine riding around on some flea-bitten donkey!'

'I don't want to ride around on him,' said the Doge's daughter. 'I want him to be my friend. I have no friends to play with, Father. You did say I could choose any one I wanted. And he's not flea-bitten at all. He's beautiful. He's much more beautiful than any of the others.'

'Don't you argue with me,' thundered the Doge. 'You could have picked the finest horse in the land and you chose that walking carpet. Look at him with his feet curled up like Turkish slippers!'

'Father,' said the Doge's daughter, her eyes filling with tears, 'if I cannot have the donkey I don't want anything.'

'All right,' said the Doge. 'If that's what you want then you will go without a present. Go back into the palace and go to your room at once.'

But the Doge's daughter ran across the square to where Jo-Jo stood and put her arms around his neck. 'Come to the palace tonight,' she whispered, 'and wait outside my window. I shall climb down and we shall run away together. Be there, Jo-Jo. Do not fail me.'

Whatever names they called Jo-Jo as his
master dragged him away through the crowds,
he did not mind. When they threw their melon
skins at him, he did not mind. For the first time
in his life, Jo-Jo was proud he was a donkey.

'Don't go getting any grand ideas inside that
ugly head of yours, you old ragbag,' his master
said. 'You're just a donkey, and a pretty poor
one at that, and don't forget it. Once a donkey,

always a donkey. And what's more you'll have no supper tonight after what you've cost me. If you'd have been a horse I'd be richer by ten thousand ducats. Do you hear me?'

Jo-Jo heard him, but he was not listening. He was making plans.

Chapter Four

JO-JO DID NOT sleep that night. He was too excited. He waited until all was quiet and then set to work. In the black of the night Jo-Jo bit through the rope that tied him to his olive tree and made his way carefully through the sleeping village, down the road and back into the city of Venice. It was a wild, wet and windy night. No one heard Jo-Jo hurrying through the empty streets, trotting over the little bridges, across St Mark's Square towards the Doge's Palace.

And then he heard the voices. At first he thought it must have been the wind whistling through the towers and spires of the city. But then he looked up. The four golden horses spoke as one, their voices a whisper on the wind, but quite clear.

'Little donkey, little donkey,' they said. 'Listen to us, little donkey. The sea is coming in. You must wake the people and warn them. Tell them to leave, little donkey. Do it quickly or it will be too late. They will drown if you do not save them. Hurry, little donkey, hurry!'

Jo-Jo galloped across the square until he reached the water's edge. He looked out over the lagoon. He could hear the waves rolling in towards him from the sea. He felt the water

washing over his hooves and saw it running
down over the stones and into the square
behind him. He lifted his head, took the
deepest breath of his life, and then he brayed
and he brayed and he brayed, until his head
ached with it.

In her bedroom in the palace, the Doge's daughter was waiting for Jo-Jo. When she heard him calling, she let herself down out of her window and ran over to him. 'Not so loud, Jo-Jo,' she said. 'You'll wake everyone up.'

And then she too heard the distant roar of the sea and heard the waves rolling in. She felt the water round her ankles and understood why Jo-Jo was braying. She knew at once what had to be done.

With the Doge's daughter on his back, Jo-Jo trotted braying through the city streets, waking everyone up.

'What?' they shouted, opening their windows and looking out into the dark streets. 'Melons at this time of night?'

'No, no!' cried the Doge's daughter. 'The sea has broken in and the city is under water. Save yourselves!'

And all the while the sea came in, flooding the square and the Cathedral and the Doge's Palace itself. Woken by Jo-Jo's braying, the people of Venice ran for their lives.

Jo-Jo the melon donkey, with the Doge's daughter on his back, guided the children and the old people to safety down the flooding streets. And all the time the waters rose round them. Houses crumbled and the great bell tower in the square came crashing down into the water.

Chapter Five

WHEN MORNING CAME they discovered that not a single life had been lost. Jo-Jo, the melon donkey, had saved the people of Venice, and they loved him for it. It was the people who asked the Doge to put up a statue, a golden statue of the melon donkey. It should stand, they said, in St Mark's Square in front of the golden horses themselves, so that no one should ever forget him.

At the unveiling ceremony the Doge placed a laurel on Jo-Jo's head and apologised for the cruel things he had said about him. 'There is a legend,' the Doge said, 'that if ever the people of Venice were in danger, the four golden horses would save them. It's a nice story, but it's just a story. It was Jo-Jo the melon donkey who saved us and we must never forget it.'

And Jo-Jo smiled secretly inside himself and was happy.

Never again was Jo-Jo made to carry anything: except, that is, for the garlands of flowers that people put around his neck whenever he went out for a walk. For he became the Doge's daughter's donkey. And he was her friend and constant companion for the rest of his life. And donkeys do live for donkey's years, you know.

If you enjoyed reading these stories,
try these tasty tales!

Jacqueline Wilson

Three
for Tea

Anne Fine

Michael Morpurgo

Three
Stories
in one

Tasty Tales
for you and me

EGMONT PRESS: ETHICAL PUBLISHING

Egmont Press is about turning writers into successful authors and children into passionate readers – producing books that enrich and entertain. As a responsible children's publisher, we go even further, considering the world in which our consumers are growing up.

Safety First
Naturally, all of our books meet legal safety requirements. But we go further than this; every book with play value is tested to the highest standards – if it fails, it's back to the drawing-board.

Made Fairly
We are working to ensure that the workers involved in our supply chain – the people that make our books – are treated with fairness and respect.

Responsible Forestry
We are committed to ensuring all our papers come from environmentally and socially responsible forest sources.

For more information, please visit our website at
www.egmont.co.uk/ethicalpublishing